BELOVED DISCIPLE

Guardian of the Holy Virgin

ROBERT JOHN HAMMOND

NEWWAY PRESS

Beloved Disciple: Guardian of the Holy Virgin
Copyright © 2025 Robert Hammond

ISBN: 979-8-9919293-3-2

Published by:
New Way Press
http://www.NewWayPress.com
Sacramento, CA 95835

Cover photo by ID 42842372 © Jozef Sedmak | Dreamstime.com

Printed in the United States of America

Contents

Acknowledgments

With deep gratitude and humility, I offer my thanks to those who walked with me on the journey of bringing *Beloved Disciple: Guardian of the Holy Virgin* to life.

To my beloved wife, Lesa—your unwavering support, constant encouragement, and sacrificial dedication made this book possible. Thank you for believing in me and in the vision behind this work, even in the quiet, unseen hours.

To Christine Gindi, whose generous feedback, thoughtful insight, and steadfast support helped shape this manuscript with both heart and clarity—your contributions have been invaluable.

To Katherine Hyde, whose professional excellence in editing and formatting brought polish and structure to these pages—your skills elevated this work with grace and care.

To Archbishop Benjamin, Father Timothy Winegar,

and Father Ian MacKinnon, thank you for your blessings, prayers, and encouragement. Your spiritual guidance and pastoral love have deeply sustained me throughout this endeavor.

And most of all, to God, to my patron Saint John the Theologian, and to the Most Holy Theotokos—thank you for your constant blessings, for guiding my steps, for protecting me through every season of life, and for calling me ever closer to the Light.

May this work bear witness to the love, mercy, and truth that endure forever.

Author's Note

*B*eloved Disciple: Guardian of the Holy Virgin is a historical novel that weaves together ancient tradition, scrip-
tural testimony, and sacred imagination to bring to life the
intertwined journeys of Saint John the Theologian and
the Most Holy Virgin Mary. While firmly grounded in
the Orthodox Christian faith, this book does not pretend
to be a scholarly or academic work. Rather, it is a work of
creative historical fiction—an attempt to recreate, through
the lens of story, the lives of these beloved saints in a cohe-
sive and emotionally resonant narrative.

The primary sources drawn upon include the New Testament—particularly the Gospels, the Acts of the Apostles, and the Book of Revelation—as well as ancient Christian writings such as the Protoevangelium of Saint James
and the Acts of John. Orthodox hymnography, including
the Akathist to Saint John the Theologian and various
canons and troparia dedicated to the Mother of God, have

also informed the portrayal of these sacred figures. Additionally, I have consulted the *Lives of the Saints* by Saint Dimitri of Rostov, various medieval traditions and legends, the Orthodox Church in America (OCA) website, and other verifiable sources, including scholarly summaries such as the biography of Saint John the Apostle found at the *Encyclopedia Britannica* (https://www.britannica.com/biography/Saint-John-the-Apostle).

Where history is silent or traditions diverge, I have employed imagination—guided by prayerful reverence and a desire to remain faithful to the spirit of Orthodox Christian tradition. My goal has been to create a cinematic and vivid retelling that honors the sacred mystery of the lives of Saint John and the Holy Virgin, drawing readers into their world and illuminating their enduring significance.

This novel does not claim to settle historical debates or to provide definitive answers. Rather, it offers a window—a narrative pilgrimage—into the early life of the Church, the bond between the Beloved Disciple and the Mother of God, and the timeless call to love and fidelity that their lives exemplify.

May this story shine a light on their memory and inspire a deeper reverence for these holy figures, whose love for Christ changed the world.

Prologue

The last light of day faded over Ephesus, casting the sky in deep hues of gold and crimson. From the hill where he sat, John could see the city below, its streets winding like veins, its great temple standing as a monument to a world he had long since left behind. The sea beyond the city stretched endlessly, its waves lapping at the shore with rhythmic constancy, a reminder of the life he'd once known—a life of nets and salt, of wind and toil. But that was before he had heard the words that would change everything.

"Follow Me."

John had followed, leaving behind all he had known, walking in the shadow of the One who spoke as no man had ever spoken, whose voice calmed the storms and whose hands brought sight to the blind. He had seen the miracles, heard the voice of the Father upon the mountain, leaned against the breast of the Master at the Last Supper. And he had remained, even when the others fled.

The memories of that day still burned within him—the cries of the crowd, the sky turning black at midday, the scent of blood in the air. John had stood at the foot of the Cross. And then, in the midst of His suffering, Jesus had looked down, His gaze piercing through the agony, and spoken the words that bound John's fate to another's.

"Woman, behold thy son."

And to him: "Behold thy mother."

From that moment, John's life had been irrevocably changed. He had taken her into his care, the one whom angels had hailed, the one who had borne the Eternal Word, the one whose heart had been pierced as she watched her Son give His life for the world. For years they had walked together, mother and son—not by blood, but by the will of the crucified Lord. In her presence, he had seen the depth of love that could endure the sword of sorrow. And in her voice, he had heard the echoes of the One who had spoken of a love greater than death.

Now she was gone.

Her passing had been peaceful, full of light and mystery, as if heaven itself had reached down and gathered her into its embrace. Her empty tomb had not surprised him. The Lord would not allow His mother to see corruption. She had been taken to where He was.

Long years had drifted by, but John carried her memory

as if it had been yesterday—a light that neither time nor exile could dim. Now, in the dusk of his life, he exhaled slowly, his fingers tracing the worn edges of the scroll before him. His task was not yet finished. The fire still burned within him, the command still lingered in his heart: to bear witness to the Word, to proclaim the love he had seen with his own eyes. He had written much, but there was still more to tell—of the beginning, of the One who was before all things, and of the mother who bore Him.

Before he could speak of what was, he must speak of what had come before.

Of the girl chosen before time, the vessel of the Incarnation. Of the mother who stood at the Cross and the Son who was given into her care.

John dipped his quill into the ink, pressing it to the parchment.

"In the beginning . . ."

CHAPTER I

The Birth of the Theotokos

The Barrenness of Joachim and Anna

The streets of Jerusalem swarmed with pilgrims, voices rising in hymns and prayers as they ascended to the temple. It was a time of celebration, of offerings and thanksgiving. But for Joachim, there was no joy in the city that day.

He stood at the temple gates, his hands trembling as he held out his offering—a gift of lambs without blemish, a sign of gratitude and devotion. But before he could enter, a voice stopped him.

"Why do you, an old man with no children, presume to offer a sacrifice to the Lord?"

The priest's words struck like a dagger. Joachim froze, the blood draining from his face.

"God has shut your wife's womb for a reason," the priest continued. "You are cursed. You have no heir."

The murmurs of the onlookers burned in Joachim's ears. His knees weakened. He clutched the lambs, his heart pounding with shame. He turned and fled from the temple, down the steps, through the crowded streets, past the laughter of fathers lifting their children onto their shoulders.

He had no son. No daughter. No one to carry on his name.

Anna was waiting when he returned home. The moment she saw his face, she knew.

"What is it?" she whispered, reaching for him.

He turned away, his voice hollow. "I cannot bear it any longer."

Tears welled in her eyes, but she did not let them fall. She had carried this sorrow for years—long nights spent in silent prayer, aching with longing. But now, the weight had become unbearable.

Joachim left that night, retreating into the wilderness. He would not return until God answered.

The Prayer in the Wilderness

Joachim wandered into the desert, his feet aching as he climbed the mountains beyond the city. Alone beneath the vast sky, he knelt upon the earth, his voice breaking in prayer.

"Lord, have You cast me away? Have I no place among Your people?"

The stars stretched silent above him. He clenched his fists, his breath ragged. "You gave a son to Abraham in his old age. You answered the prayer of Hannah and gave her Samuel. Will You not hear me?"

For forty days and nights, Joachim fasted. He wept. He cried out to God, his soul pouring forth like a river. And then, on the fortieth night, the heavens stirred.

A great light shone upon the mountain. Joachim shielded his eyes as a voice, strong and radiant, called his name.

"Joachim, do not fear."

He fell to his face, trembling.

"The Lord has heard your prayer. Your wife shall conceive and bear a daughter, and through her, salvation will come to the world."

The light faded, and the night was still once more. But Joachim knew—God had spoken.

He rose, his strength renewed. He would return home.

The Annunciation to Anna

Anna knelt in the garden, her tears watering the dry earth. She had prayed for so long. Would God ever hear her?

A sudden breeze stirred the air. The leaves rustled. A golden light descended, and before her stood an angel, clothed in radiance.

"Anna, the Lord has seen your sorrow."

She gasped, drawing back, her hands trembling.

"You shall bear a daughter, blessed above all women. Through her, the world shall be saved."

Anna pressed a hand to her lips, her heart racing. "A child? In my old age?"

The angel smiled. "Nothing is impossible for the Lord."

Then, just as swiftly as he had come, he was gone.

Anna stood up, her breath catching in a sob. She lifted her hands to the sky. "My soul magnifies the Lord, for He has looked upon His servant in her lowliness."

At that moment, Joachim appeared at the garden gate. Their eyes met, and they knew.

God had answered.

The Birth of the Theotokos

Nine months passed, and the time came for Anna to give birth. It was a night of stillness. A soft rain fell upon the earth, the scent of fresh myrrh drifting on the air. Within their home, the cry of a newborn broke the silence.

Joachim knelt beside Anna, his eyes wet with wonder. "A daughter," he breathed.

The midwife lifted the child, swaddled in linen. She was radiant, her tiny face serene, her dark eyes wide and filled with light.

Anna reached for her, pressing her against her heart. "Her name shall be Mary," she whispered.

Outside, the rain ceased. A single star shone brighter

than the rest, casting a silver glow upon the house of Joachim and Anna.

The Theotokos had entered the world.

The Prophecies of Her Destiny

Word of the miraculous birth spread. In the temple, the high priest Zechariah received a vision: the infant Mary, chosen before all time, was destined to bear the Redeemer.

Like the patriarchs who waited for the promise afar off, Simeon lingered in the desert, burdened by the weight of centuries. Three hundred years had passed since the Word of the Lord first came to him, yet his heart had not faltered. In the hush of night, as stars wheeled overhead, the voice returned, clear and unwavering: "You will not see death until you behold the Lord's Christ."

And in distant lands, the Wise Men studied the stars, unaware that the sign they sought had already entered the world.

The Hymn of the Angels

As Anna held her newborn close, a soft melody filled the air, though no musicians played.

The angels sang.

"Rejoice, O full of Grace, the Lord is with thee! Blessed art thou among women and blessed is the Fruit of thy womb!"

Anna wept with joy, her heart full.

The child stirred, her tiny fingers curling around Anna's own. The one who would bear the Savior had come.

CHAPTER 2

The Presentation of the Theotokos in the Temple

The Three-Year-Old Child Who Climbed the Temple Steps

The streets of Jerusalem bustled with life as the morning sun cast golden light upon the towering walls of the temple. Merchants called out their wares, the scent of burning incense mingled with the crisp air, and the sound of footsteps echoed against the stone pathways. The city was alive with pilgrims and priests, all moving toward the sacred heart of Israel's worship. At the entrance of the temple courts, a small group gathered—a husband and wife, their faces alight with reverence, guiding a child no more than three years old toward the House of the Lord.

Joachim and Anna walked slowly, their hands resting on the shoulders of their daughter. Between them, Mary stepped forward with quiet confidence, her small feet barely making a sound against the stone road. She was no longer a babe in arms—she was three years old, yet she carried herself with a grace that did not belong to the very young.

Anna's heart was filled with joy, though it was mixed with sorrow. She had waited so long for this child, had prayed through long nights for her arrival. And now she was leading her away, offering her to God as she had promised. It was a vow she had made before the child was even conceived.

"Do you understand, my child?" Anna whispered. "Today, we give you to the Lord."

Mary lifted her eyes—deep, knowing eyes that shone like stars. She nodded. "I am ready."

Joachim squeezed his wife's hand, affection and reverence in his gaze. They had known since her birth that Mary was unlike any other child. Even the way she looked at the world, the way she spoke and carried herself—it was as though she saw beyond what others could perceive.

The steps of the temple loomed before them. The great doors stood open, revealing the high priests waiting within. Among them was Zechariah, a righteous man who had been given a vision of this very moment. He had stood in the Holy of Holies and heard a voice foretelling the coming of the one who would bear the Messiah.

And now, here she was.

The child paused at the base of the stairs. Anna drew a

sharp breath. Would she hesitate? Would fear make her falter?

But without a word, Mary lifted the hem of her robe and began to climb.

The people gasped. It was a steep ascent for one so small. But she did not stumble, did not look back. Her tiny feet touched each step with quiet certainty.

And when she reached the top, she turned toward her parents, a smile on her face, and raised her hands in farewell.

Anna wept. Joachim placed a steadying hand on her shoulder, though his own eyes glistened.

"She belongs to the Lord," he murmured.

The Life of the Theotokos in the Temple

The high priests received the child with reverence, sensing the holiness surrounding her. Zechariah himself took her by the hand and led her past the great altar, past the golden lampstands, and into the chambers where she would dwell.

She would not be raised among other children. Instead, Mary would grow up within the very heart of the temple, dwelling in the inner sanctuaries where only the priests were permitted to go. It was unprecedented. Yet none questioned it, for the presence of God surrounded her like a mantle.

The priests observed her in wonder. She did not behave as other children did. She spent hours in prayer, her small hands lifted in supplication. The words of the psalms were on her lips before she had even been taught them. At times, they would find her standing in silent contemplation, her face radiant with unseen light.

And when she ate, she did not partake only of the food given to her by the priests. She was fed by the hand of an angel.

It was whispered in hushed voices. Some had seen it. A figure robed in light descending to the child as she knelt in prayer, offering her bread that was not of this world. None could explain it, but all knew what it meant.

The hand of God was upon her.

The Songs of the Angels

At night, as the city of Jerusalem slept, the halls of the temple were filled with the sound of voices.

Not the voices of men, but the songs of angels.

The priests, keeping their vigils, would pause in their prayers, turning toward the chamber where Mary slept. They heard the melodies, soft and reverent, words of praise beyond human comprehension. And in the midst of the song, the child's voice would rise, singing with them, lifting her praise to the Lord.

What child was this who could hear the voices of the angels?

Only the one chosen before all time.

The Vision of the High Priest

Years passed, and the child grew in wisdom and beauty. She was unlike any other maiden in Jerusalem. Her eyes held the depth of the heavens. Her hands, small and delicate, were always raised in prayer. She was gentle, yet her presence was like fire—radiant, powerful, untouched by the corruption of the world.

And then came the day when Zechariah, now aged and filled with the Spirit of the Lord, received a vision.

As he stood in the Holy Place, offering incense, a voice called his name.

"Zechariah."

He turned, his heart pounding.

Before him stood an angel, clothed in light.

"The time is near," the angel said. "She who was promised will soon be called forth."

Zechariah fell to his knees. "What must be done?"

The angel stretched out his hand. "She must be given to a guardian, for soon the Lord will overshadow her, and she shall bear the Savior of the world."

Zechariah bowed his head. He understood. The child who had climbed the temple steps alone was destined to bear the Word made flesh.

CHAPTER 3

The Betrothal and the Annunciation

The Chosen Guardian

The temple had been Mary's home for nearly a decade. From the time she was three years old, she had dwelt within its sacred courts, growing in wisdom, purity, and prayer. The priests marveled at her devotion, her ceaseless longing for God. Yet the day had come when she could no longer remain. The Law of Israel dictated that a young woman could not dwell in the temple beyond her twelfth year.

A council of priests gathered in the temple, their voices hushed with reverence. The high priest, clad in his sacred vestments, stood at the altar, lifting his hands in prayer. "O Lord, show us the one whom You have chosen to guard the Virgin of the Lord."

Then an angel appeared before him, radiant in the glow of the golden lampstands. "Gather the unmarried men of the house of David," the angel instructed. "Let them each bring a staff, and to whomsoever the Lord shall show a sign, he shall be her guardian."

Messengers were sent throughout Judea, summoning righteous men of David's lineage. Among them came Joseph of Nazareth, an elderly carpenter, a widower with sons of his own. Though he had not sought this honor, he obeyed the call.

The staffs of the men were gathered and laid before the altar, and the priests cast lots to determine who would be chosen. As they prayed, a miracle unfolded—one of the staffs bloomed before their eyes. A white lily burst forth from its barren wood, filling the air with a fragrant sweetness.

Then, as the priests stepped back in awe, a dove emerged from the staff, alighting upon Joseph's head. A hush fell over the temple. The sign was undeniable.

The high priest turned to Joseph. "You have been chosen by the Lord to take into your care the Virgin of the Lord."

Joseph took a step back, his hands trembling. "I am an old man," he said. "I have sons older than she is. I am not worthy."

The high priest shook his head. "It is the will of God."

Joseph knelt before Mary, his voice barely above a

whisper. "I am unworthy," he said. "But I will protect you with my life."

And Mary, full of grace, simply bowed her head. "I am the handmaid of the Lord."

The Spinning of the Veil

Though Mary now dwelt in Joseph's house, she remained devoted to the temple, spending her days in prayer and quiet labor. One day, the priests called for a new veil for the Holy of Holies, and they summoned the purest virgins of David's line to take part in the sacred weaving.

Lots were cast to determine who would spin each color—gold, blue, scarlet, and purple. Mary was chosen to spin the scarlet and true purple.

She returned home in silence and took up her spindle. Between her fingers, the fibers drew out in a fine, glistening thread, as if they carried a mystery not yet spoken into the world. The spindle turned with gentle rhythm, and her labor, though simple, became a quiet offering. Each thread was spun with care, unwinding like a prophecy—scarlet and purple, colors of kingship and sacrifice—woven not yet into cloth, but into the very fabric of what was to come. The weaving would follow in its season, but already the thread was touched by the shadow of a great mystery.

The Angelic Visitation

Mary took up her water jar one evening and went to the well to draw water. The sky was deepening into twilight, the first stars glimmering in the heavens. As she bent over the well, a voice called out:

"Hail, you who have received grace! The Lord is with you; blessed are you among women!"

Mary froze. The voice was unlike any she had ever heard—a voice that echoed with eternity. She turned, searching for the speaker, but no one was there. A shiver ran down her spine.

Trembling, she picked up her water jar and returned home to resume her work on the veil. But as soon as she sat down, a great light filled the room.

Before her stood the Archangel Gabriel, his form shining with uncreated light.

"Fear not, Mary," the angel said gently, "for you have found favor with God. Behold, you shall conceive in your womb and bring forth a Son, and you shall call His name Jesus. He shall be great and shall be called the Son of the Most High. The Lord God shall give Him the throne of His father David, and His kingdom shall have no end."

Mary's eyes glistened in wonder. "How shall this be, seeing I know not a man?"

"The Holy Spirit shall come upon you," Gabriel replied, "and the power of the Most High shall overshadow you. Therefore, the Holy One to be born of you shall be called the Son of God. And behold, your cousin Elizabeth has also conceived a son in her old age, for nothing is impossible with God."

A silence fell over the room. The moment stretched into eternity.

Then Mary lifted her gaze, her voice steady.

"Behold the handmaid of the Lord. Be it unto me according to thy word."

At that moment, the Word became flesh within her womb.

The angel departed, and Mary, filled with awe and trembling with joy, rose and set out for the hill country—to the house of Elizabeth.

The Visitation

Mary's journey to the house of Elizabeth and Zechariah was long, the road winding through rugged hills. Yet an unseen joy carried her forward.

When she reached the house, she knocked, and as soon as Elizabeth heard her voice, she cried out:

"Blessed are you among women, and blessed is the fruit of your womb! And why is this granted to me, that the mother of my Lord should come to me? For behold, when the voice of your greeting reached my ears, the babe in my womb leaped for joy!"

Mary's heart swelled with understanding. She lifted her voice in praise:

"My soul magnifies the Lord, and my spirit rejoices in God my Savior . . ."

She remained with Elizabeth for three months, helping her in her final days of pregnancy. But as Mary's own condition became more evident, she wondered. What would Joseph say? What would the people do?

She journeyed back to Nazareth, her faith unwavering, yet her future uncertain.

The Burden of Joseph

Days passed, and Joseph noticed the change. The glow in Mary's face. The quiet peace that surrounded her. And then—the unmistakable swelling of her abdomen.

His heart pounded. What was he to do?

He was a righteous man. He could not accuse her, could not have her stoned. But how could he take her as his wife when she carried a child that was not his?

That night, as he wrestled with his sorrow, a voice called to him in his dreams.

"Joseph, son of David, fear not to take unto thee Mary thy wife, for that which is conceived in her is of the Holy Spirit. She shall bring forth a Son, and thou shalt call His name Jesus, for He shall save His people from their sins."

Joseph awoke with a gasp. He fell to his knees before Mary. "Forgive me. I did not understand."

"You were chosen, Joseph," she whispered. "You are not alone in this."

From that moment, he renewed his vow to protect her with his life.

The Test of Bitter Waters

But rumors began to spread. The priests, bound by the Law, summoned Joseph and Mary to appear before them. Joseph stood before the high priest, his hands shaking.

"Give up the virgin whom you received out of the temple of the Lord," the priest demanded.

Tears welled in Joseph's eyes. He had feared this moment. He had feared what men would say, what they would do.

The priest prepared the bitter waters—a mixture of holy water and dust from the temple floor, a test prescribed in the Law. If they had sinned, the water would bring forth affliction.

Joseph took the cup, closed his eyes, and drank.

The silence in the temple was suffocating as he was sent away into the wilderness. When he returned, he was unscathed.

Then Mary took the cup in her hands. Without hesitation, she drank.

And she, too, remained unharmed.

Gasps spread through the gathering. The priest's eyes widened. "If the Lord God has not made manifest your sins, neither do I judge you."

He sent them away in peace.

Joseph took Mary's hand, and they returned home, rejoicing and glorifying the God of Israel.

The Journey to Bethlehem Awaits

Then, a decree went out from Caesar Augustus that all the world should be registered.

Joseph prepared for the journey. Bethlehem awaited.

Prophecy would soon be fulfilled.

CHAPTER 4

The Nativity of Christ and
the Flight into Egypt

The night was silent, save for the soft whisper of the wind sweeping over the hills of Bethlehem. The journey had been long, the roads difficult, but at last, Joseph led the Virgin Mary toward shelter. Yet the city was overflowing with travelers, and no home had room for them. The doors remained shut.

Joseph clenched his jaw as he glanced at Mary, who, despite the weariness of the road, bore no complaint upon her lips. He knew the time was near. The hour of the child's birth had come.

The inns were full, their doors closed, but providence guided them another way. A villager, moved by a quiet mercy he could scarcely name, offered them a cave beyond the busy streets—a shelter where beasts found rest from the night. It was no random hollow, but a place prepared from the foundation of the world, rough and hidden, awaiting this hour. Joseph led Mary there with gentle hands. The stone walls pressed close, the air thick with the scent of earth and straw. A stillness deeper than silence filled the cave, as if the very breath of heaven hovered there unseen. In that sacred hush, where human eyes saw only poverty, Light stirred beneath her heart. And as in a cave He would one day rise from death, so now, in a cave, He would be born—clothed in humility, crowned in mystery, while angels watched in reverent awe.

The Birth in the Cave

Mary sat upon the straw, her face serene. There was no furrowing of pain upon her brow, no cry of distress. As she closed her eyes, a great light filled the cave, so bright that Joseph, who had stepped outside in search of aid, shielded his face and fell to his knees in awe.

The very fabric of time seemed to pause.

The light grew in brilliance, enveloping the cave in a radiance not of this world. Then, just as suddenly as it had come, it receded. And there, in the quiet aftermath of the divine radiance, the infant Christ lay in His mother's arms, His eyes wide and filled with wisdom beyond the ages.

He did not cry but rested peacefully at the breast of the Virgin Mary.

Joseph turned at the sound of hurried footsteps. A

midwife had finally come, too late to assist but drawn by the strange hush that clothed the night. She stepped into the cave and stood still, caught within a silence deeper than words—a silence that seemed to cradle the very breath of the world.

Mary sat in stillness, the newborn Child resting peacefully in her arms. No trace of pain marked her face, no weariness touched her. Around her, the cave walls gathered the hush like a shelter, rough and ancient, as if the earth itself had curved inward to hold the moment. Beyond the entrance, the stars stood watch, their quiet fires kindled against the darkness, a thousand distant lamps shining softly. Above them, unseen but near, the angels waited, their song held in the quiet, the first note poised. They waited for the cry—the cry that would rise like the first break of dawn, casting a narrow, tender path through the shadows, a road that would carry both joy and sorrow in its wake.

THE CHILD'S BREATH stirred faintly, His chest rising and falling with the fragile rhythm of life newly entered into time. Beneath the swaddling cloths, His heartbeat whispered—the infinite wrapped in humility, eternity resting within the frailty of flesh.

The midwife gasped and sank to her knees, overcome

not only by sight but by the trembling weight of what she could not name. It was not merely a birth she had witnessed, but a love so vast it could only be held in silence.

"My soul has been magnified this day," she whispered, her voice no more than a breath, "for my eyes have seen the salvation prepared before the world began."

Trembling, she rose and stepped from the cave, where Salome stood waiting beneath the wide, listening sky.

"Salome, Salome," she cried, clutching her hand, "I have seen a wonder beyond all telling. A virgin has given birth. The stars are hushed, the earth holds its breath, and the angels wait. They wait for His cry—the cry that will break the silence and set the long road shining before Him. Nothing will ever be the same."

Salome stepped into the cave and approached Mary. The Blessed Virgin looked upon her without fear, knowing well that the works of the Lord were beyond human reasoning.

Salome fell to her knees, tears streaming down her face. "Have mercy on me!" she sobbed.

And the infant Christ, still resting in His mother's arms, turned His gaze upon her.

She wept, but this time in joy. "Blessed is the God of Israel, for He has visited His people!"

⁊❧

The Shepherds and the Magi

In that same hour, out in the fields, shepherds tending their flocks beheld the heavens burst open in a blaze of celestial light. A voice like rushing waters called out to them:

"Fear not! For behold, I bring you good tidings of great joy, which shall be for all people. For unto you is born this day in the city of David a Savior, who is Christ the Lord."

A multitude of angels filled the sky, their voices ringing in an unearthly harmony: "Glory to God in the highest, and on earth peace, goodwill toward men!"

The shepherds wasted no time. They ran to the cave, falling to their knees before the newborn King. Their rough hands trembled as they beheld Him, wrapped in swaddling cloth, lying in a manger.

Not long after, a new star blazed in the heavens, guiding three wise men from the east. When they arrived, they too fell in worship, offering their gifts:

Gold, for the newborn King.

Frankincense, for the Son of God.

Myrrh, for the sacrifice He would one day endure.

The Virgin Mary watched in silence, pondering all these things in her heart.

The Flight into Egypt

But in the halls of power, darkness stirred. Herod, upon hearing from the wise men of the birth of a new king, was filled with rage. He sent out his soldiers to slay every male child in Bethlehem, hoping to destroy the promised one.

That night, as Joseph slept, an angel of the Lord appeared to him in a dream.

"Arise! Take the child and His mother and flee to Egypt, for Herod seeks to destroy Him."

Joseph woke with a start. Without hesitation, he gathered what little they had, wrapped the child in warm cloth, and led the Virgin Mary away from the city. They traveled by night, slipping into the wilderness, the angel's warning heavy upon them.

The road was treacherous, the dangers many. Wild animals roamed the desert, thieves lurked among the hills. One night, as they neared the Egyptian border, a band of robbers emerged from the shadows.

Their leader, Gestas, sneered as he stepped forward. "Give us what you carry," he demanded, eyeing the gold, frankincense, and myrrh.

But another man, standing beside him, hesitated. Dismas.

His gaze fell upon the Virgin Mary, upon the child nestled in her arms. And something stirred within him.

"Let them go," Dismas said. "Take my silver instead." He lifted up his bag of silver that he had taken from the previous robberies.

Gestas scoffed but did not argue. He snatched the silver from Dismas and turned away.

As the Holy Family passed, Mary looked upon Dismas, her expression filled with something beyond gratitude—a knowing. And she said softly:

"The Lord will remember you."

Dismas did not understand the weight of her words then.

But years later, as he hung upon a cross beside the same child now grown, he would whisper, "Lord, remember me when You come into Your Kingdom."

And the promise would be fulfilled.

CHAPTER 5

The Early Life of
Saint John the Theologian

Birth of John, Son of Thunder

The waves of the Galilean sea crashed upon the rocky shore as the cries of a newborn filled the house of Zebedee. The child, red-faced and strong, was placed into the arms of his mother, Salome. She gazed at the tiny boy, her heart swelling with love and an understanding that this child would be set apart.

Zebedee, a fisherman of Capernaum, watched as Salome whispered over their son's head, "His name shall be John."

She had seen it in a dream—a vision of her child standing in the midst of light, speaking words that made the heavens tremble. She did not understand the meaning of it, but she knew the Lord had a purpose for her son.

The boy grew, strong in body and quick in mind. From an early age, he walked along the shores with his father and older brother James, learning the ways of the fishermen. He heard the waves in the night, whispering ancient secrets, and watched the stars wheel overhead, wondering what lay beyond them.

A Mother's Influence

Salome was more than a fisherman's wife. She was a woman of deep faith, one whose devotion shaped the hearts of her children. She had stood witness to divine mysteries before. Some believed she was the same Salome who had been present at the birth of the Virgin Mary and even at the Nativity of Christ.

This was the faith she instilled in her sons. Though they were raised by the sea, accustomed to the weight of nets and the scent of salt in the air, their hearts were open to the call of God. When she first heard of the man preaching in the wilderness, clothed in camel's hair and crying out for repentance, she knew her sons must hear him.

The Voice in the Wilderness

The years passed, and John became a young man, his hands calloused from casting nets, his feet accustomed to the shifting sands. He was drawn to the synagogues, hungry for the words of the prophets, for the promises yet to be fulfilled. He spoke little, but when he did, his voice carried an intensity that made others listen.

Then came the rumors. A prophet had arisen in the wilderness. A man clothed in camel's hair, his voice like thunder, calling the people to repentance.

John left his nets behind.

He and his brother James traveled beyond the Jordan to see this prophet with their own eyes. When they arrived, they saw the man standing in the waters, the crowds gathered on the banks, hanging on his every word.

John the Baptist.

His voice rang out over the river. "Repent! For the kingdom of heaven is at hand!"

John stood frozen. This was no ordinary prophet. He was like Elijah returned, a voice crying out in the wilderness. And when he spoke of the One who was to come, something within John burned like fire.

The Baptist saw him watching from the crowd. Their eyes met, and for a moment, John felt as if the prophet could see straight into his soul.

"You will see Him soon," John the Baptist said, his voice low, meant only for him.

John's eyes glistened. "Who?"

"The Lamb of God."

And then, one day, He came.

The Call of the Fisherman

It was an ordinary morning on the shores of Galilee. The sea was still, the dawn light just beginning to crest over the horizon. John and James worked alongside their father, casting their nets, waiting for the catch. The rhythmic splash of water, the weight of the nets in their hands—it was all they had ever known.

Then came the voice.

"Follow Me."

John turned, his fingers still curled around the woven strands of the net. A man stood before him, His eyes unlike any John had ever seen—deep and endless, like the waters of the sea, yet filled with something more. A presence so powerful, yet gentle, as if eternity itself moved within Him.

Jesus.

John had heard of Him. The rabbi from Nazareth. The healer. The teacher. The One whom John the Baptist had pointed to with awe, declaring, "Behold, the Lamb of God, who takes away the sins of the world."

And now He stood before him.

Jesus stepped closer, His gaze never leaving John's. Then, He reached out and rested His hand lightly on John's shoulder. The touch was firm, steady—not just an invitation, but a calling. Something stirred deep within John's soul, a recognition beyond words.

"Come," Jesus said, His voice both an invitation and a command. "Follow Me, and I will make you fishers of men."

John looked at his brother. James's hands were already loosening their grip on the nets. He did not hesitate. He did not question. He *knew*.

The weight of the nets, the salt in the air, the pull of the sea—none of it mattered anymore.

Without a word, John dropped the nets.

And followed.

The Sons of Thunder

John and James walked at the Master's side, eager and full of youthful zeal. Jesus spoke of things no rabbi had ever taught. He spoke as One who had authority, as if the words of the prophets had taken flesh and walked among them.

John watched Him heal the sick, calm the storms, and cast out demons with a word. But what astounded him most was His love. A love so deep, so fierce, that it shattered the hardness of men's hearts, drawing even the most broken to Him.

One day, as they traveled through a Samaritan village, the people refused to receive Jesus. John felt his blood rise with indignation.

"Lord," he said, his voice edged with fire, "shall we call down fire from heaven to consume them?"

Jesus turned to him. There was something in His gaze—both correction and deep affection.

"You do not know what spirit you are of," He said gently. "For the Son of Man did not come to destroy men's lives, but to save them."

John's face burned with shame, but he understood.

Jesus had called him and his brother Boanerges—Sons of Thunder. He knew their fiery passion, their boldness, but He also saw something deeper in John.

And He was shaping him for something greater.

The Beloved Disciple

John remained close to Jesus in all things. He listened more than he spoke, taking in every word, every lesson. When others questioned, John simply trusted. When others hesitated, John followed.

At the Last Supper, it was John who reclined against Jesus' chest, the one closest to His heart. And when Jesus said, "One of you will betray Me," it was John whom Peter turned to, silently pleading for him to ask who the betrayer would be.

But John's story was only beginning. The fire within him had not faded—it had only been transformed. His passion had not been extinguished—it had been refined.

And soon, the fire of Pentecost would fall, and John would rise as the Apostle of Love.

CHAPTER 6

John's Journey with Christ

The Miracle at Cana

The sun hung low over the hills of Galilee as the wedding guests gathered in the courtyard of a house in Cana. The air buzzed with laughter, the clinking of cups, the melodies of flutes and lyres. The fragrance of roasted lamb and fresh bread filled the air. It was a day of celebration, and among the invited guests was Jesus of Nazareth, along with His mother, Mary, and His new disciples.

John stood beside James, drinking in the scene. He had followed the Master for only a short time, but already he felt the world shifting around him. Jesus spoke little of Himself, but John sensed something vast and deep beneath every word He uttered, as though the sky itself waited in anticipation of His voice.

Then a whisper passed through the crowd.

"The wine has run out."

John saw Mary move toward Jesus, a quiet urgency in her step. She leaned in and spoke softly. Though John could not hear her words, he saw Jesus glance toward the worried servants, then back at His mother.

"Woman," He said gently, "what does this have to do with Me? My hour has not yet come."

Mary did not argue. Instead, she turned to the servants and said simply, "Do whatever He tells you."

Jesus rose and walked to the large stone water jars, each big enough to hold gallons of water for purification. The servants hesitated as He gestured toward them.

"Fill the jars with water."

They obeyed. John watched, breathless, as the jars were filled to the brim. Then Jesus said, "Now draw some out and take it to the master of the feast."

One of the servants scooped from a jar and carried the cup to the steward. The man sipped, his brows lifting in astonishment. He turned to the bridegroom.

"Everyone serves the good wine first," he said, shaking his head in wonder. "But you have kept the best until now!"

John felt a shiver run through him. This was not the work of an ordinary rabbi. Something had changed in the air, as though creation itself had bent toward Jesus' will.

It was only the beginning.

&

The Raising of Jairus's Daughter

John saw many miracles in those days. The sick were healed, the blind received sight, the demons fled at His command. But it was on the day when a desperate father pushed through the crowd that John's heart nearly stopped.

Jairus, a ruler of the synagogue, fell at Jesus' feet, his face streaked with tears. "My little daughter is dying," he pleaded. "Come and lay Your hands on her, so she may be healed and live."

Jesus nodded, and they set out at once. The crowd pressed around them, eager, hopeful, whispering of what they might see. Then, as they walked, a messenger arrived.

"Do not trouble the Teacher any longer," the man said solemnly. "Your daughter is dead."

A murmur of sorrow rippled through the crowd, but Jesus only turned to Jairus and said, "Do not be afraid—only believe."

John followed as they reached the house, stepping inside with Jesus, Peter, and James. The wailing of mourners filled the air. Jesus looked at them and said, "Why do you weep? The child is not dead but sleeping."

Laughter—sharp, bitter—broke out among the mourners. But Jesus paid them no mind. He took the child's hand and whispered, *"Talitha koum."*

Little girl, arise.

John's chest tightened as the child's eyes fluttered open.

She sat up, looking around in confusion. Her mother gasped, rushing to her side, clutching her to her chest.

"She is alive," John whispered, awestruck.

Jesus smiled, stepping back. "Give her something to eat."

The room erupted in joy. But John only stared at Jesus, feeling as though he had stepped beyond the veil of time itself.

Who was this Man, that even death obeyed Him?

The Mount of Transfiguration

The night was cool as Jesus led Peter, James, and John up a high mountain. They had climbed in silence, their footsteps crunching softly against the rock. John did not know why they had come. But when Jesus stopped, He turned to them with an expression John could not describe.

Then, before their eyes, He changed.

His garments shone white as the sun; His face blazed with a light so brilliant that John was forced to shield his eyes. It was as if the heavens had broken open and revealed His true nature.

Then, suddenly, they were not alone.

Two men stood beside Jesus, their robes glistening with the same unearthly light. Though John had never seen them before, he knew them in an instant.

Moses.

Elijah.

The Law and the prophets, speaking with the One who fulfilled them both.

Peter fell to his knees. "Lord, it is good that we are here! Let us build three tabernacles—one for You, one for Moses, and one for Elijah!"

But even as he spoke, a cloud descended over them, thick and radiant. And a voice came from within it:

"This is My beloved Son. Listen to Him."

John's body trembled. He knew that voice. The voice that had called light into existence, the voice that had thundered from Sinai, the voice that had spoken to the prophets.

The voice of the Father.

And as suddenly as the wonder had begun, it was over. The light faded. The cloud lifted. And only Jesus remained, standing alone.

He looked at them gently. "Do not be afraid."

They fell at His feet, overcome.

As they descended the mountain, Jesus warned them, "Tell no one what you have seen, until the Son of Man has risen from the dead."

John did not understand what He meant. But he knew this—he had seen the glory of God.

The Road to Jerusalem

John followed Jesus everywhere, through the streets of Galilee, into the homes of sinners and tax collectors, across the storm-tossed sea. He saw thousands fed with a few loaves and fish, saw demons flee at a word, saw lepers cleansed with a touch.

But he also saw something else.

A shadow.

Jesus spoke more and more often of what was to come. He told them that He must suffer, that He must die. John recoiled at the thought. He did not want to believe it.

Yet the road led only one way.

To Jerusalem.

To the cross.

And John, though afraid, would follow Him there.

CHAPTER 7

The Betrayal

The Last Supper

The upper room was dimly lit by the glow of oil lamps. The scent of warm bread, bitter herbs, and spiced wine lingered in the air, mingling with the tension that hung between the disciples. The table was set simply—dishes of bean stew, olives, fish sauce, dates, and unleavened bread. This was not the Passover meal itself but the supper before it, the last they would share together before everything changed.

John sat closest to Jesus, as he always did, leaning against Him as they shared their final meal. He could feel the slow, steady rhythm of the Master's breathing, but beneath it, there was a weight—a sorrow that could not be spoken.

Jesus took the bread, lifted His eyes toward heaven, and blessed it. Then, He broke it, passing it to them. "Take, eat; this is My body."

John hesitated for only a moment before taking a piece, feeling the weight of those words settle deep in his soul. He did not understand fully, but he knew this was something sacred, something that would change everything.

Then Jesus took the cup, the deep red wine catching the flickering light. "Drink from it, all of you. For this is My blood of the new covenant, which is poured out for many for the forgiveness of sins."

The silence in the room was deafening. John's fingers tightened around the cup as he brought it to his lips. The warmth of the wine spread through him, but it was not just wine. It was something more—something eternal.

Jesus' gaze swept across the table. "One of you will betray Me."

A murmur rippled through the room, disbelief and unease settling over them. John felt Peter's hand on his arm, a silent plea. *Ask Him.*

Leaning in close, John whispered, "Lord, who is it?"

Jesus dipped a piece of bread and handed it to Judas. "It is he with whom I dip this bread."

Judas took the bread, his fingers clenching around it. A shadow flickered across his face, and in an instant, he stood, the woven mat beneath him shifting slightly. Without a word, he turned and stepped away, his sandals whispering against the stone floor as he vanished into the night.

The weight in John's chest grew heavier. The air in the

room had changed. He could not name it, but he felt it—
something was ending. Something was beginning.

The Betrayal in Gethsemane

The night air in Gethsemane was thick with tension, the
scent of olive trees mingling with the cold bite of approach-
ing dawn. John had never seen Jesus look so burdened, His
face drawn with an agony that no words could express.
Even Peter, always brash and unshaken, was restless beside
him. The Master had warned them, but still they did not
understand.

Then the flickering glow of torches cut through the
darkness. A company of soldiers, their armor glinting,
moved swiftly toward them. At their head was Judas.

John's breath hitched. He had hoped—prayed—that it
would not come to this.

Judas stepped forward, his face unreadable, his movements slow, deliberate. The weight of what he was about
to do hung over him like a storm cloud. He leaned in and
pressed a kiss to Jesus' cheek.

"Rabbi," he murmured.

Jesus did not flinch. "Judas, do you betray the Son of
Man with a kiss?"

Before John could move, the soldiers surged forward, hands grasping for Jesus. Peter reacted first. His
sword flashed in the torchlight, and a cry rang out as the
blade struck its mark. Malchus, the high priest's servant,

stumbled back, clutching his ear, blood spilling through his fingers.

"Enough!" Jesus' voice cut through the chaos. He reached out and touched Malchus, and in an instant, the wound was gone. The soldiers hesitated, their grip momentarily slackening. But then, as if recalling their orders, they seized Him.

John stood frozen, his heart hammering. The others ran. Even Peter, who had moments ago raised his sword, disappeared into the shadows.

But John could not leave Him.

CHAPTER 8

The Road to Golgotha

The streets of Jerusalem swelled with an angry tide. The sun beat down on the stone-paved roads, its heat suffocating, yet a chill of dread settled in John's bones. He pushed forward through the swelling crowd, staying close, his heart pounding.

Jesus staggered beneath the weight of the cross. His body, flayed by the scourging, trembled with each labored step. Blood soaked His tunic, dripping onto the dust-covered ground. The soldiers prodded Him onward, their whips lashing against His torn flesh whenever His knees buckled.

The air was thick with mockery, the jeering voices of the mob mingling with the cries of weeping women who trailed behind. John saw the Theotokos among them. She had wrapped her veil tightly around her face, but nothing could hide the anguish in her eyes.

Then Jesus collapsed.

The Roman centurion cursed, motioning for one of the onlookers to step forward.

"You!" he barked, grabbing the arm of a man in the crowd.

The man hesitated, his dark eyes shifting from the soldiers to Jesus, then back again. He was Simon of Cyrene, a foreigner who had come for the Passover pilgrimage.

"Take up the cross," the centurion ordered.

Simon's jaw tightened, but he obeyed. He shouldered the rough wood, lifting the burden that had nearly crushed the Man before him. Jesus, gasping for breath, pushed Himself up from the ground and continued walking.

John moved closer, keeping pace.

Further along, a woman suddenly broke from the crowd. She ran toward Jesus, a piece of cloth in her hands. John recognized her—Veronica. She reached out, pressing the cloth gently against His face, wiping away blood and sweat.

A soldier moved to shove her back, but Jesus caught her gaze, something unspoken passing between them. When Veronica pulled the cloth away, her hands trembled. Imprinted upon the fabric was the face of Christ, serene even in suffering.

John barely had time to process the wonder before the soldiers forced them forward.

The city walls thinned as they approached the outskirts—the Place of the Skull.

Golgotha.

The name whispered through John's mind like an omen.

Here, condemned men were sent to die. But this place was no ordinary execution ground.

It was said that beneath the rocky hill lay the burial place of Adam himself. The first man, whose sin had brought death into the world, was buried beneath the very place where redemption would be accomplished.

As they reached the summit, the executioners moved with brutal efficiency. The crosses were laid out. The condemned were stripped of their outer garments. Jesus, beaten and broken, was cast down upon the rough-hewn wood.

John turned away for just a moment—just a breath—before the hammer struck.

A cry of pain, deep and raw, cut through the air.

John clenched his fists as the nails pierced through Jesus' wrists, fastening Him to the beams. Each strike of the mallet sent a shockwave through his soul. The cross was lifted, its base wedged into the rock.

The Son of God hung between heaven and earth.

And the world darkened.

CHAPTER 9

The Words that Changed Everything

The unnatural gloom deepened, swallowing the city in shadow.

Even the most hardened soldiers shifted uneasily. The midday sun had vanished, leaving only an eerie twilight. The air was thick, almost suffocating, as if creation itself recoiled from what was unfolding.

John barely noticed the crowd anymore. His gaze was fixed only on the cross.

To the left and right of Jesus, two criminals hung upon their own crosses. Their bodies trembled with agony. One of them, Gestas, spat bloodied curses into the air. "If You are the Christ," he sneered, "save Yourself and us!"

But the other thief—Dismas—turned his head, his face contorted not with anger, but with something else.

"Do you not fear God?" he rasped. "We are justly condemned, for we receive what we deserve. But this Man has done nothing wrong."

A silence stretched between them. Then, in a voice scarcely more than a whisper, Dismas turned to Jesus.

"Lord, remember me when You come into Your kingdom."

John remembered.

The name Dismas—he had heard it before. A story told long ago.

During the Flight into Egypt, when the Holy Family fled from Herod's wrath, they had encountered a band of robbers. Among them were two young men—Gestas and Dismas.

They had searched the travelers, their hands greedy for riches. But Dismas had faltered. He looked upon the child Mary carried in her arms, and something stirred in him—a conviction he could not explain.

He stopped the others. "Let them go," he said. "Take my silver instead."

And before they departed, he whispered a plea to the infant: "O most blessed of children, if ever a time should come when I should crave Thy mercy, remember me and forget not what has passed this day."

And now, here Dismas was—hanging beside that very Child, who had become the suffering King.

Jesus turned His head, His swollen eyes locking onto

Dismas's. His lips parted, and with divine certainty, He spoke:

"Truly, I say to you, today you will be with Me in Paradise."

John exhaled.

Even now, in agony, Jesus saved.

His gaze flickered downward.

The Theotokos stood there, her hands clenched, her face pale but unwavering.

John's heart twisted. He wanted to shield her from this horror, but he knew she would not leave.

Then, through the darkness, Jesus spoke again.

"Woman, behold thy son."

His mother lifted her head, her sorrow-filled eyes meeting John's.

Jesus' gaze then turned to John, though His strength was fading.

John barely heard the jeering crowd now; all of creation seemed to hold its breath. The voice of his Master, hoarse with agony yet steady with love, reached him through the wind: "Behold your mother."

A trembling overtook John's limbs—not fear, but the weight of divine trust settling upon him. The Mother of God turned her eyes upon him, the depths of her sorrow vast as the sea, yet within them an unwavering submission to the will of her Son. John bowed his head. The sky darkened further. A wind rose, swirling dust and whispered prayers around them. At that moment, he understood: from this day forth, he would not only be the beloved disciple, but the protector of the Mother of God herself.

Thunder rumbled in the distance.

Jesus lifted His eyes toward the heavens.

"It is finished."

The ground trembled. The veil of the temple was torn from top to bottom. The great curtain, once a barrier between man and the Holy of Holies, now hung in two tattered halves, its fine threads unraveling in the darkness.

Scarlet and purple fibers—the very colors spun long ago by the hands of the Virgin Mary—danced in the air like falling embers. She had woven that veil in her youth, never knowing that one day it would be torn asunder at the death of her Son.

The earth groaned, splitting open.

John fell to his knees as a great cry rang out from the Roman centurion nearby.

"Truly, this was the Son of God!"

A hollow silence followed, broken only by the wind that howled through the darkened sky.

John looked up at the cross one final time.

The lifeless body of Jesus hung limp, His head bowed.

The world had changed.

Forever.

CHAPTER 10

The Myrrh-Bearer and the Beloved Disciple

Salome, Mother of the Sons of Thunder

Long before the Resurrection, before the Cross, before the miracles and the storms calmed by a single word, there was a woman—a mother—who knelt beside the waters of Galilee, watching over her two sons as they played in the surf.

Salome, first cousin of the Theotokos, had been raised in the household that had cared for Christ Himself, and though she had married the fisherman Zebedee and borne two sons—James and John—her heart remained ever drawn to the mysteries of God.

It was no surprise that when her sons left their father's fishing boat to follow the Messiah, she followed too.

Salome was among the women who traveled with Jesus,

providing for His needs, listening to His teachings, and witnessing the miracles. She was there when her sons were named the Sons of Thunder, their zeal burning brightly beneath the authority of Christ.

And she was there when the earth shook, when the sky turned black, when blood and water poured from His side.

The Morning of the Empty Tomb

The night had been endless, filled with the echoes of grief and unanswered questions.

But as the first light of dawn broke over Jerusalem, Salome, along with Mary Magdalene and Mary, the mother of James, prepared to go to the tomb. The spices in their hands were meant for burial. Their hearts still bore the weight of despair.

John had told her what he had seen. The last moments. The final words. "Behold thy mother." But she had been helpless to comfort him. She could barely comfort herself.

The road to the garden was silent, except for the sound of footsteps upon the earth.

Then—

A quake.

The ground trembled beneath them. The air was thick with something unseen, something powerful. The guards at the tomb, Roman soldiers hardened by war, fell like dead men.

And the stone—

It had been rolled away.

Salome clutched the spices tighter, her breath coming fast. The entrance yawned open before them, dark and gaping.

And then, a voice.

"Why do you seek the living among the dead?"

The angel stood before them, clothed in radiance, his face shining with something not of this world.

"He is not here. He is risen."

The jars fell from her hands. The sound of shattering clay echoed across the garden.

They ran.

Salome's feet barely touched the ground as she raced toward the house where the disciples were gathered. She burst into the room, the words tumbling from her lips, disjointed, wild.

"He is risen! The tomb—it is empty! We saw an angel!"

But their words were met with doubt. The men exchanged glances.

Until John and Peter pushed past her and ran.

She followed in their wake, heart hammering, mind racing. And when she arrived at the tomb once more, she saw John standing frozen at the entrance—Peter stepping inside—and then at last—John himself entering.

The burial cloths lay there. The face covering was folded.

The tomb was empty.

And then Salome glorified the Risen Lord.

Breakfast by the Sea

Days passed in a strange haze of wonder and confusion. Jesus had appeared to the disciples, but everything still felt like a dream.

And so, when Peter turned to the others one night and said, "I am going fishing," they all agreed.

They returned to the familiar, to the Sea of Galilee, to the life they had left behind.

But the night's work was fruitless. The nets remained empty, the sea yielding nothing to them.

John sat near the stern of the boat, staring out across the dark water, lost in thought. Was this it? Were they to return to the old life as though nothing had happened?

Then, as the first light of dawn broke over the water, a figure appeared on the shore.

A voice called out. "Children, have you any food?"

Peter sat up, startled. "No," he called back.

The voice came again. "Cast the net on the right side of the boat, and you will find some."

John felt something shift in his chest, a deep stirring of recognition.

They cast the net—and suddenly, it was full. So full they could barely pull it in.

John turned to Peter, his voice barely more than a whisper.

"It is the Lord."

Peter didn't hesitate. He grabbed his outer garment,

threw it on, and plunged into the water, swimming for the shore.

John stayed in the boat, hands gripping the net, his heart racing. The others rowed the boat toward land, dragging the weight of the catch behind them.

And when they reached the shore, they saw it—

A fire.

Fish already laid upon it.

And Jesus.

He stood there, waiting for them.

"Bring some of the fish which you have just caught," He said.

Peter, still soaked, rushed to the net and dragged it to land—153 fish in all. Yet the net did not break.

Jesus turned to them. "Come and eat."

They gathered around, the fire crackling, the warmth of the meal pressing against the chill of the morning air. No one dared to ask Him who He was. They knew.

Jesus took the bread, breaking it as He had so many times before. He gave it to them. And likewise gave them the fish.

John watched Him, memories flooding his mind.

The feeding of the five thousand.

The night He had walked upon the sea.

The hands that had once been pierced now offering them food.

This was the third time He had appeared to them since rising from the dead.

And then, after they had eaten, Jesus turned to Peter.

"Simon, son of Jonah, do you love Me more than these?"

Peter's breath hitched. "Yes, Lord, You know that I love You."

"Feed My lambs."

A second time—

"Simon, son of Jonah, do you love Me?"

Peter swallowed hard. "Yes, Lord; You know that I love You."

"Tend My sheep."

A third time—

"Simon, son of Jonah, do you love Me?"

Peter's face crumpled.

"Lord, You know all things; You know that I love You."

Jesus met his eyes, and His voice was gentle.

"Feed My sheep."

John sat in silence, watching the exchange, understanding its weight.

Then Peter turned, glancing at him. He pointed toward John and asked, "But Lord, what about this man?"

Jesus' gaze settled on John, His voice steady.

"If I will that he remain till I come, what is that to you? You follow Me."

The words sank deep into John's soul.

And thus the saying spread among the brethren—that the disciple whom Jesus loved would not die.

But John knew what Jesus meant.

John was not called to death. He was called to witness.

To testify.

To live on, carrying the light of the Resurrection to the world.

And in the end, to write the words that would stand for all eternity—

"And there are also many other things that Jesus did, which if they were written one by one, I suppose that even the world itself could not contain the books that would be written."

Amen.

CHAPTER II

The Descent of the Holy Spirit & the Mission of Saint John

The upper room was silent, save for the steady breathing of the disciples.

It had been fifty days since the Passover, ten since Jesus had ascended into heaven. Though He had promised the Comforter, though they had witnessed miracles beyond imagination, still they waited.

John sat near the Virgin Mary, her presence as steady as it had been beneath the Cross. She, more than any of them, understood the power of waiting, the mystery of God's timing.

Then—

A sound.

A rush of wind, filling the room, shaking the very walls.

John felt the air surge around him, a fire igniting in his chest.

Tongues of flame descended upon them, not burning, but filling them with power.

John gasped as his mind flooded with understanding, words forming on his lips in a language he had never spoken.

Across the room, Peter rose to his feet, his face alight with something fierce, something unstoppable.

The doors burst open.

The Birth of the Church

The crowds in Jerusalem, gathered for the feast, turned at the sound of voices pouring from the upper room—words in every tongue, spoken by Galileans. Wonder swept through them.

"What does this mean?" they asked one another, some in awe, others scoffing.

Peter stepped forward, his voice thundering above the crowd. "Men of Judea, listen to my words!"

John watched, awestruck, as Peter spoke with boldness he had never seen before. This was not the man who had trembled before a servant girl, denying Christ three times. This was a man filled with the Spirit of God.

Peter proclaimed the fulfillment of prophecy, the coming of the Messiah, the power of Christ's Resurrection. His words pierced the hearts of those who listened.

"What must we do to be saved?" they cried.

"Repent and be baptized," Peter declared, "every one of you, in the name of Jesus Christ for the forgiveness of your sins, and you shall receive the gift of the Holy Spirit."

That day, three thousand souls were baptized, and the Church was born.

John's heart swelled as he witnessed the first fruits of Christ's promise. The Spirit that had spoken through the prophets now burned within them.

The Death of Stephen

Saul of Tarsus, a zealous Pharisee, sought out those who followed Christ, dragging them from their homes, casting them into prison.

And then came Stephen.

A deacon, full of the Holy Spirit, unafraid to speak the truth before the Sanhedrin. Stephen was dragged beyond the city gates, the mob seething with rage.

Stephen lifted his eyes to the heavens, his face shining with something otherworldly. "Behold, I see the heavens opened, and the Son of Man standing at the right hand of God."

A stunned silence fell over the crowd. For a moment, the fury in their eyes was replaced with something else— uncertainty, perhaps even fear. But then, as if possessed by some unseen force, they cried out with one voice and rushed upon him.

The first stone struck Stephen's temple, blood trickling down his cheek. Another crashed against his ribs, forcing him to his knees.

John, standing among the believers in the city, heard the news before he saw the crowd returning. His heart clenched. The memory of another unjust trial, another innocent man sentenced to die, came rushing back to him. Christ had stood in silence before Pilate; now Stephen knelt before the fury of the people. He could almost hear Jesus' voice: "Father, forgive them, for they know not what they do."

As Stephen collapsed under the onslaught, he raised his hands toward the sky, his voice steady despite the pain. "Lord Jesus, receive my spirit."

Stephen's blood darkened the earth, but his final words rose to the heavens. "Lord, do not hold this sin against them."

Then silence.

John's heart ached as he heard the news. Yet as he lifted his eyes toward the heavens, he knew—Stephen had not been abandoned. The same Christ who had ascended before their eyes had stood to welcome him home.

A Gathering Storm

The persecution only intensified. The followers of Christ were driven from synagogues, cast out from families, and hunted by those who saw them as blasphemers. Yet the faith did not wane—it grew.

John continued his mission, his words drawing crowds, his presence a symbol of the faith that would not be silenced. But the cost was rising.

One by one, his brethren faced the weight of the empire. The name of Christ was on every tongue—some in devotion, others in condemnation.

John watched, prayed, and waited. He had seen the crucifixion, the empty tomb, the tongues of fire at Pentecost. He had seen Stephen fall, and many others after him.

And he knew—the storm had only begun.

CHAPTER 12

Flight to Ephesus

THE MISSION EXPANDS

The night sea was restless. Waves churned beneath the moonless sky, their whitecaps illuminated only by the faint glow of distant stars. The creaking of wood and the howling wind filled the ears of those aboard the small ship, a vessel barely fit for such a journey. The salt stung John's lips, but he did not notice. His hands gripped the railing, his eyes fixed on the horizon, his heart steady but expectant.

The Theotokos stood nearby, her veil billowing in the wind. Though she was calm, John could see the weight she carried. She had left Jerusalem without hesitation when the warnings came, yet she had not spoken of sorrow nor of fear. Only once had she turned to him, her voice quiet but resolute: "He wills it."

John did not doubt it. But still the sea was rising.

A violent gust slammed into the ship, sending it lurching. Cries rose from the crew as they scrambled to secure the mast, their voices barely audible above the storm. Prochoros, John's trusted scribe and disciple, clung to the side, his knuckles white.

"Master," he called out over the wind, "this storm—it is unnatural!"

John knew. He had seen many tempests in his years as a fisherman, but this was different. The darkness was deeper, the wind wilder, as if something unseen raged against them.

The ship rocked violently, and a wave crashed over the deck, sweeping two men off their feet. John stumbled forward, grasping for anything solid, his hands finding the mast. He turned toward the Theotokos. She had not moved.

Another wave. This one larger. A wall of water surged toward them, its crest higher than the ship itself. It struck with thunderous force.

The world tilted.

Then silence.

John opened his eyes to darkness. Cold, consuming darkness. Water surrounded him, filling his ears, pressing against his chest. He had been thrown into the depths. The sea had swallowed him whole.

He reached out, but there was nothing. No up, no down,

only the crushing weight of the abyss. His lungs burned. He had seen death before—watched it claim his Lord on the Cross. Now it was coming for him.

He closed his eyes.

And then, light.

It did not come from above or below but from within. A warmth spread through him, dispelling the cold. A voice—not his own, yet deeply familiar—whispered in his soul.

"Fear not."

His body surged upward, drawn not by his own strength but by something unseen. The weight of the sea fell away. Then—air.

John broke through the surface, gasping. The storm had not ceased, but something had changed. The waves, though high, no longer threatened to crush him. The wind, though fierce, seemed somehow restrained. The ship was still afloat, battered but whole. And upon the deck, the Theotokos stood, unshaken, her eyes searching the water.

She found him.

With strength beyond reason, John swam toward the ship. Hands reached down, pulling him aboard. He collapsed onto the deck, his breath ragged, his limbs shaking.

Prochoros knelt beside him. "Master..."

John held up a hand. He turned to the Theotokos. "How?" he managed, his voice hoarse.

She did not answer at first. Then, gently, she spoke. "He wills it."

The storm passed before dawn.

৯৬

THE SHORES OF EPHESUS welcomed them with golden light spilling across the horizon. The city, grand and sprawling, pulsed with life. Temples rose high above the streets, their marble columns gleaming in the sun. Statues of pagan gods loomed over the marketplace, their cold, unseeing eyes casting shadows upon the people below.

John felt it the moment he stepped onto the land. Darkness lingered here. Not the kind that came with the setting sun, but a deeper shadow, one that clung to the hearts of men, binding them in unseen chains.

He turned to the Theotokos. "It is as He said."

She nodded. "Then we must begin."

Word spread quickly. Some had heard of them—of the miracles, of the name of Jesus. Others saw only troublemakers, men who defied the order of things. It was not long before they were summoned.

The high priests of Artemis sat upon carved thrones, their robes adorned with gold and crimson. Incense curled into the air, thick with the scent of sacrifice. The chief priest, his face lined with age and arrogance, studied them with calculating eyes.

"You come preaching a new god," he said. His voice was like the hiss of a serpent.

John met his gaze. "Not new," he replied. "From before the world was made."

A murmur rippled through the chamber. The priest's expression darkened. "Blasphemy. Artemis is the great mother, the queen of heaven. Your words are poison."

John took a step forward. "The Light has come into the world," he said, his voice unwavering. "And the darkness has not overcome it."

The ground trembled beneath their feet.

A cry rose from outside. The temple doors burst open, and a man stumbled in, his body wracked with convulsions. His eyes rolled back, his lips forming soundless words. The priests recoiled in horror.

John stepped toward him. The man fell to his knees, his body shaking violently.

John knelt beside him. "You are free," he whispered.

A final shudder, then stillness. The man opened his eyes. Clarity returned.

He wept.

The silence in the temple was absolute. Then, without a word, John turned and walked out. The Theotokos followed. Prochoros hurried after them, his hands gripping the parchment he had carried since their arrival.

"You must write this," John said to him that night as they sat beneath the flickering oil lamp. "Write all of it."

Prochoros hesitated. "All of what, master?"

John closed his eyes. The words came, not from himself, but from the One who had called him long ago.

"In the beginning was the Word, and the Word was with God, and the Word was God."

Prochoros froze mid-breath. He dipped his quill into the ink.

And he began to write.

CHAPTER 13

The Fall of Artemis

TRIUMPH OF THE TRUE GOD

The city of Ephesus had never known a night so restless. The temple of Artemis, one of the wonders of the world, stood as a symbol of divine power, its colossal columns rising into the heavens, its priests confident in the goddess's eternal rule. Yet whispers filled the air—whispers of a man whose words had shaken the very foundation of their worship. The Apostle John had come.

His teachings had fanned out like embers caught in the wind, and the people, once devoted to the goddess, had begun to abandon the rituals and sacrifices. The silversmiths, whose trade depended on the idols of Artemis, raged at their loss of wealth. The temple priests feared for their dominion, and the city trembled on the edge of chaos.

The Confrontation

John stood in the great marketplace, his voice calm yet filled with authority. "Men of Ephesus, you see with your own eyes that these gods are no gods at all. They are fashioned by the hands of men, lifeless and powerless. But the One I proclaim is the Living God, He who created heaven and earth."

The crowd was divided—some listened, their hearts stirred, while others clenched their fists, unwilling to let go of their traditions. The temple priests, furious, stepped forward.

"You blaspheme Artemis, whom the whole world worships!" one of them shouted.

John did not waver. He lifted his gaze toward the great temple, his expression unmoved. "If she is a god, let her defend herself."

Murmurs rippled through the crowd. Some priests scoffed, but others hesitated, as if uncertain whether John's words carried more weight than they dared admit.

Then the earth trembled.

The Collapse of the Idol

A low rumble shook the ground beneath them. Gasps rose from the people as cracks splintered through the marble foundation of the temple. The great doors groaned, as if under some unseen force, and suddenly, from within the sanctuary, there was a deafening crash.

A priest screamed. The colossal statue of Artemis—gilded and towering—had cracked at its base. With a terrible roar, the idol tilted forward, then collapsed entirely, shattering upon the sacred floor.

Silence followed. Then wailing.

Some of the priests fell to their knees in horror. Others fled, their faith crumbling along with the statue. Women wept, clutching broken pieces of the idol in their hands, as if willing the goddess to return to them. The silversmiths and merchants, seeing their wealth now reduced to dust, tore at their robes in despair.

But among the people, another sound rose—whispers of awe, of revelation. Some fell to their knees, not in mourning, but in prayer, turning their hearts toward the God whom John had proclaimed.

The Rage of the Priests

Not all were willing to accept the truth.

The high priest of Artemis, his face twisted with fury, turned upon John. "You have done this!" he shouted. "You and your sorcery!"

John's expression remained composed. He had not moved, had not raised his hands, had not uttered a single curse or incantation. And yet the idol had fallen. The temple itself had betrayed its emptiness.

"I have done nothing," John said, his voice steady. "It is

your own gods who have fallen before the power of the Almighty."

In desperation, the priests and craftsmen seized stones, hurling them toward John. But before they could strike him, a great wind surged through the square, knocking them to the ground. Some scrambled away, terror gripping their hearts. Others, overcome with fear, abandoned their faith in Artemis entirely.

The people stood still, caught between their past and their future. And then, one by one, voices rose.

"Tell us more of this Jesus," a woman called from the crowd.

Others echoed her words, and in that moment, the balance shifted. The temple of Artemis, once the pride of Ephesus, had lost its hold.

The Triumph of Christ

That night, John gathered those who had turned away from Artemis, and he preached to them of the true and living God. The temple still stood, but its power had been shattered. No priest dared to rebuild the idol. No silversmith dared to make new statues. The people knew—

Artemis had fallen, but Christ remained.

John stood beneath the moonlit sky, watching as the fires in the temple flickered low. He had known, even before setting foot in Ephesus, that the power of Christ would triumph. He had not needed to raise his voice in anger, nor strike the temple walls, nor call upon heaven to make a sign.

The truth itself had been enough.

As he turned away, leading the people toward the light of the Gospel, the winds carried his final words across the empty square:

"The kingdoms of this world shall pass away, but the kingdom of our Lord shall endure forever."

CHAPTER 14

The Prophecy of Mount Athos

The wind carried whispers across the sea. It moved like a living thing, tugging at the sails, twisting around the mast, howling through the rigging with an unnatural force. The ship groaned beneath it, tilting precariously as waves slammed against its hull. The sailors, seasoned men hardened by years of braving the Aegean, cast anxious glances at the sky, at the roiling black clouds devouring the horizon. This was no ordinary storm.

John stood at the bow, his hands gripping the wooden rail. The scent of the salt air mingled with something else—something he could not name but felt in the marrow of his bones. Beside him, the Theotokos stood silent, her veil lifting in the wind, her eyes fixed on the darkness ahead.

"Master," Prochoros called, bracing himself against the shifting deck. "We cannot outrun this."

John did not answer. He turned to the Mother of God, waiting, knowing that she had seen what they had not.

She exhaled softly, then spoke. "This is not a storm of the sea."

The sailors stirred at her words, fear creeping into their expressions. A shout rang out from the stern—one of the men had seen something in the water. A flickering, spectral glow beneath the waves, moving with them, circling like a predator. John felt it too—a presence that did not belong to wind or water.

The sea did not rage against them.

Something else did.

A sudden crack of thunder split the heavens. The ship heaved as the waves rose higher, and for a moment, John thought the sea itself might swallow them whole.

Then she stepped forward.

The Theotokos lifted her hands and spoke no words, but the power that flowed from her was unmistakable. The very air shifted. The storm, which moments before had seemed unrelenting, paused, as if it had been struck dumb by her presence. The howling wind stilled. The waves lost their fury. The black clouds overhead shuddered, then began to break apart, revealing the golden light of the sun.

The ship righted itself. The sea was calm once more.

The sailors fell to their knees. Even Prochoros, who had seen much, could only stare in awe.

The island appeared before them, bathed in the glow of dawn. Athos.

೭ง

THE LAND FELT untouched by time. Towering cliffs rose from the water's edge, crowned with lush forests and meadows that stretched into the distance. The scent of wildflowers and cypress filled the air. Birds wheeled high above, their cries piercing the stillness that lay over the land like a veil.

As they stepped onto the shore, a strange sensation washed over John. It was as if something unseen watched them—not with hostility, but with expectation. The earth beneath his feet felt sacred, though no temple stood here. Not yet.

The Theotokos walked ahead of them, her gaze scanning the landscape. Then she paused.

"This place is chosen."

John felt the words settle in his chest, heavy with meaning. He stepped forward. "For what, my Lady?"

Her lips curved in the smallest of smiles. "For what is to come."

A shudder rippled through the ground, so subtle it might have been missed by any other. But John felt it. So did Prochoros. The sailors, who had been murmuring amongst themselves, froze as a deep, guttural sound echoed through the hills.

A rumble. Then a crack.

The mountain shook.

Farther inland, past the tree line, something was breaking. Stone split. Wood groaned. The cry of something unseen carried through the air, high and shrill. And then, in the distance, they saw it.

A shrine, crumbling before their very eyes. Marble columns, once pristine, now cracked and falling. A great idol, shaped in the likeness of an ancient god, toppled from its pedestal, shattering against the earth with a sound like thunder.

The sailors crossed themselves in fear and awe. John turned to the Theotokos, understanding now.

"The false gods fall before you."

She inclined her head. "Not before me," she murmured, "but before the One I bear."

John gasped as he felt something shift in the air. A vision—not seen with his eyes, but within his soul. He saw Athos, not as it was now, but as it would be. He saw figures robed in black, their heads bowed in humility, their lips moving in unceasing prayer. He saw towers rising from the land, domes gleaming in the light of the sun. He saw incense drifting through ancient halls, heard the echo of chants that would not cease until the world itself faded into eternity.

A place untouched by time. A garden not for man, but for God.

"This land will be a beacon," the Theotokos said. "A refuge for those who seek the Kingdom. Here men will lay aside the world and seek only His face. Here the prayers of the righteous will rise like incense, unbroken until the final day."

John dropped to one knee, overwhelmed. The weight of history—of eternity—pressed upon him. He could see it all. The monks, the saints, the unyielding devotion that would be rooted in this place. A holy mountain, guarded by the prayers of those yet to be born.

A second Eden.

The Theotokos turned her eyes to the sky. "This is my garden," she whispered. "And it shall be forever."

THE JOURNEY BACK was silent. The sailors, once skeptical men of the sea, now cast sidelong glances at the Theotokos with something bordering on reverence. Prochoros sat near the stern, parchment spread before him, his quill moving swiftly, capturing all that had transpired.

John sat beside him. "Write it well," he said softly.

Prochoros nodded. "I will."

The wind carried them forward, gentle now, guiding them with unseen hands. John turned back, watching as the mountain receded into the distance. But he knew, with certainty, that it would never fade from the mind of God.

Mount Athos had been claimed.

And its destiny was only beginning.

CHAPTER 15

The Dormition of the Theotokos

The house in Jerusalem where the Theotokos dwelled was filled with an atmosphere of quiet reverence. The apostles, gathered from the corners of the world, had come at the prompting of the Spirit, knowing in their hearts that their beloved mother's time on earth was drawing to a close. She had been a pillar of strength for them, the silent presence of unwavering faith after Christ's Ascension. Now, as they looked upon her serene face, they felt a sorrow they had not known since Calvary.

John remained at her side as he had since the Lord had entrusted her to him. Her presence had been his refuge, a living testament to Christ's love. But now her body was frail, her breath light as a whisper. Yet even in her weakness, she radiated a peace unlike anything of this world. The air seemed to shimmer around her as if heaven itself was drawing near.

One evening, as John sat beside her, the Theotokos looked upon him with deep affection. "My child," she said softly, her voice like the hush of a breeze through olive leaves, "the time has come for me to go to my Son. Do not mourn, for I shall not leave you truly. I shall pray for you always."

Tears welled in John's eyes, but he nodded. He had always known this day would come, yet his heart ached at the thought of parting from her.

The apostles gathered around her bed, and Peter, with trembling hands, anointed her forehead with oil. The fragrance of myrrh filled the room, and as they prayed, the very air seemed to change. A golden light descended, brighter than the glow of the lamps, and the room was filled with a heavenly radiance. Voices unseen chanted in a language beyond mortal tongues. The walls of the house seemed to fade, and the apostles felt as though they were standing at the threshold of eternity.

With one last breath, a sigh as gentle as the falling of a leaf, the Theotokos closed her eyes. Her soul was carried away in that divine light, and for a moment, time itself seemed to stop.

The apostles knelt in silence, overcome by the holiness of what they had witnessed. Then Peter spoke, his voice breaking through the stillness. "She is not dead," he said, his eyes shining with tears. "She has merely fallen asleep."

The Burial and the Miracle of the Withered Hand

Following Jewish custom, the apostles prepared her for burial, though none could bring himself to think of her as dead. With reverent hands, they carried her body in procession to the tomb near Gethsemane, the same garden where Christ had prayed before His Passion. As they walked, a luminous cloud hovered above them, and celestial hymns echoed in the air.

Yet not all in Jerusalem looked upon this moment with reverence. A certain Jewish priest, resentful of Christ and His followers, regarded the funeral procession with disdain. He moved forward, his heart hardened, determined to overturn the bier upon which her body rested.

As he reached out his hand to grasp the sacred vessel of her body, a sudden force struck him. He cried out in pain. His arm had frozen in place, withered and useless.

The crowd gasped, some stepping back in fear, others falling to their knees in astonishment. The apostles, still carrying the bier, halted, watching in silence.

The priest groaned, his eyes wide with terror as he realized his sin. He fell to his knees, tears streaming down his face. "Forgive me!" he cried. "I did not know . . . I did not understand . . . Holy Mother of the Lord, have mercy on me!"

At that moment, the apostles, filled with compassion, prayed over him. Peter stepped forward, raising his hands to heaven. "Lord, who showed mercy even from the Cross, heal this man that he may know the power of Thy Mother's intercession."

And as the priest wept, his withered arm was suddenly restored, flesh and sinew knitting together before the astonished eyes of all. Overcome with awe and repentance, he knelt and kissed the feet of the Theotokos where she lay upon the bier, weeping for joy.

From that moment, he became a follower of Christ, telling all who would listen of the power of the Theotokos, the Mother of the Lord.

The Arrival of Thomas and the Vision of Glory

Three days later, a hurried knock came at the door. John rushed to open it, and there stood Thomas, breathless and grief-stricken. "Where is she?" he asked, his voice trembling. "I was on my way, but the ship was delayed. I prayed to see her one last time."

The apostles led Thomas to the tomb, but as they rolled away the stone, they gasped.

It was empty.

The burial shroud remained, folded neatly where her body had been placed, but she was gone.

A hushed awe fell upon them all. Then Thomas, still weeping, fell to his knees. "I saw her," he whispered. "As I traveled here, a vision appeared before me. She was surrounded by light, lifted into the heavens by angels. She smiled upon me and said, 'Do not weep, for I am with my Son, and I am with you always.'"

A great wonder filled their hearts. It was as if the tomb had never been meant to hold her, as if earth itself had yielded her to heaven.

John turned his gaze upward, tears streaming down his face. He had lost her in body, but he knew she had not truly left them. The Theotokos, the Mother of the Church, had entered into glory, and from that moment on, she would be their unfailing intercessor.

The Everlasting Presence

The apostles remained in Jerusalem, their sorrow transformed into joy. The faithful soon learned of the miracle, and the place of her empty tomb became a site of pilgrimage. A sweet fragrance lingered in the air where she had once rested, and miracles were reported by those who prayed at the site.

John, now more than ever, felt her presence guiding him. Though the years would pass and trials would come, he knew the Theotokos was watching over them all.

And so, even in her Dormition, she continued her work—not as one departed, but as one ever-living, always interceding, forever the Mother of all who called upon her Son.

CHAPTER 16

Confrontation with Sorcery &
Exile to Patmos

The name of John had reached the highest seats of power in Rome. The Apostle of Love, as the faithful called him, had become a danger to the empire—not by sword or rebellion, but by the Word of God, which spread like wildfire in the hearts of those who heard him.

From Ephesus, his teachings had reached across Asia Minor, and the temples of the old gods had begun to crumble—not by force, but because the people abandoned them. In desperation, the priests and rulers sought to silence him. And so John was seized, bound, and brought to Rome to stand trial before the emperor himself—Domitian, who ruled with an iron hand and viewed the growing Christian faith as a threat to his divine authority.

The Poisoned Cup

The crowd gathered in the forum, eager for spectacle. The officials had spread the word that the so-called prophet from the East would face the judgment of the gods.

John stood before them, wrists bound in front of him but face serene, his eyes reflecting a peace that unsettled his accusers. Emperor Domitian leaned forward, scrutinizing the old man before him. He was unlike any other prisoner Rome had taken. There was no fear in him. No trembling.

A priest of the old gods stepped forward, holding a chalice in his hands.

"If you serve the true God, let Him save you," the priest sneered. He turned to the emperor. "This is a deadly poison. One sip is enough to kill."

The emperor smirked, intrigued. He nodded for the test to proceed.

With hands still bound, John lifted the cup to his lips. He closed his eyes, whispering a prayer, then drank. The liquid burned down his throat, but his body did not weaken. His breath remained steady. He did not falter.

The priest's confidence faltered instead. He waited. The crowd murmured.

John lifted his gaze. "The Lord is my portion and my cup. He upholds my life."

The emperor's amusement faded. He was not accustomed to defiance—especially not from a man nearing ninety winters, whose frail frame and weathered face spoke of a life long spent. Yet there was a light in the old man's eyes that unsettled even the most hardened of rulers. Domitian narrowed his eyes and gave a signal.

"Prepare the cauldron."

The Boiling Oil

John was led through the streets, the mob pressing close, eager to witness the next test. A great bronze cauldron was prepared, filled to the brim with boiling oil. The heat radiated from it, distorting the air like waves over a desert.

The guards bound John's hands behind him, leading him up the steps. The executioner hesitated only for a moment before shoving him forward.

The apostle fell into the oil.

A collective gasp rose from the crowd. Some turned away, unable to stomach the sight. Others leaned in, expecting the screams, the writhing agony.

But there was none.

John stood within the oil as though it were cool water. The flames licked the sides of the cauldron, but they did not touch him. His body did not burn; his skin did not blister. He raised his hands, now free of their bindings, and lifted his eyes toward the heavens.

A cry of fear rippled through the spectators. The executioners, frozen in place, stumbled backward. The Roman soldiers, men who had seen death in countless forms, turned pale.

Some dropped their weapons, their hands trembling. Others crossed themselves instinctively, whispering prayers to gods they were no longer certain could hear them. A few, overcome with terror, fled from the scene, their sandals slapping against the stone streets as they vanished into the city's shadows.

"The gods are against us," someone whispered.

"No," another voice said, trembling. "It is his God."

The emperor, who had remained seated in detached amusement, now rose to his feet. His smirk was gone, his expression unreadable. His lips parted as if to speak, but no words came. He swallowed hard, glancing at his advisors, as if expecting one of them to explain what had just occurred.

The silence stretched. Then a general stepped forward, his face pale, his voice low. "If we attempt to kill him again, my lord, we risk offending the gods—or worse, proving his God is greater."

The emperor clenched his fists, unwilling to accept what his eyes had seen.

"This man cannot be killed," the centurion muttered.

The emperor's gaze flickered to John, standing unharmed before him. Killing John would not silence him; it would make him a legend. If the people believed his God had saved him, then his following would only grow.

But exile—exile would remove him from the world.

"Send him to Patmos," the emperor said at last, his voice hoarse. "Let him speak to the waves and the rocks. Let him see how much power his god has there."

The Journey to the Island

The ship cut through the dark waters, the wind whipping against the sails as the island of Patmos loomed on the horizon. John stood at the stern, watching as the city of Rome faded into the distance.

He had been cast away, sent to a desolate rock to die forgotten. But as the waves crashed around him, he knew—this was not the end.

The Spirit was not bound by chains. The Word of God was not silenced by distance. The Lord had not abandoned him.

The Sorcerer Kynops

Patmos was not empty. Among its inhabitants was a man named Kynops, a sorcerer known for his dark arts and demonic power. The people feared him, believing he could control the seas and summon spirits at his will.

When John arrived, the news of his miracles and teachings spread even to Kynops, who scoffed at the notion of this old man's God. Seeking to humiliate him, Kynops gathered the people of the island and stood before John.

"Old man," he sneered, "do you truly think your God is greater than my power?"

John looked upon him with pity. "You serve the prince of lies, but his power is fleeting. The light of Christ scatters all darkness."

Kynops laughed, raising his arms toward the sky. At his command, the waters of the sea began to churn violently. The islanders gasped in terror as waves rose unnaturally high, crashing against the cliffs.

But John remained unmoved. He lifted his hands in prayer, his voice rising above the storm. "Lord of all creation, let the power of darkness be cast down."

At once, the raging waters stilled. The wind ceased. A deathly silence fell over the island.

Kynops's laughter faltered. His face twisted in rage. "I will show you true power!" he bellowed, stepping toward the water's edge.

But before he could utter another word, the sea surged forward. A mighty wave rose, engulfing him in an instant. The people cried out as the sorcerer was pulled beneath the surface, swallowed by the very forces he claimed to command.

The waters settled once more. Kynops was never seen again.

The people of Patmos fell to their knees in fear and awe, crying out to John. "Tell us of this God who is greater than the power of demons!"

And so, on that forsaken island, the gospel took root.

John turned his face to the heavens. His exile was not a punishment. It was a calling.

For soon the heavens would open, and the mysteries of the ages would be revealed.

CHAPTER 17

Revelation on Patmos

DIVINE VISION

The island of Patmos lay silent beneath the vast expanse of the heavens, the waves crashing against the rocky cliffs in rhythmic, eternal motion. The night was still, save for the rustling of olive trees swayed by the wind. But within a small cave nestled amid the craggy landscape, the silence was broken.

John knelt in prayer, his hands trembling as they rested on the cold stone floor. His body had grown frail with age, his beard streaked with white, yet his spirit burned with unquenchable fire. The night pressed around him, but within, a great stirring arose.

Suddenly, the air in the cave thickened. A great light erupted, golden and terrible, its brilliance forcing John to shield his eyes. His breath came in short gasps. Though he was already kneeling, an unseen weight pressed upon him, bowing him even lower until he lay prostrate on the stone.

The cave vanished. The world around him dissolved into blinding radiance, and John felt as if he were no longer bound to the earth. He was caught up—his body? His spirit? He did not know. Only that he was carried beyond time, beyond sight, beyond all human understanding.

The Alpha and the Omega

A voice like the roar of many waters thundered through the vastness.

"I am the Alpha and the Omega, the First and the Last. Write what you see in a book and send it to the seven churches."

John turned, and before him stood One like the Son of Man, clothed in a robe that flowed like living light, girded with a golden sash. His face burned like the sun at its peak, His eyes like flames of fire, His voice shaking the foundations of the heavens.

John's knees buckled. The very sight of Him was unbearable. He fell as though dead, his body trembling with the force of divine majesty.

A hand touched his shoulder—firm, yet full of tenderness.

"Do not be afraid."

John dared to lift his eyes.

"I am He who lives, and was dead, and behold, I am alive forevermore. And I have the keys of Death and Hades."

A scroll appeared in His hands, sealed with seven seals. Around Him the heavens stirred, and suddenly, John saw beyond the veil of time.

The Breaking of the Seals

The voice of an angel called forth, "Who is worthy to open the scroll and break its seals?"

A silence fell—deep, eternal. None in heaven, nor on earth, nor under the earth was worthy.

John felt sorrow pierce him. Was there none to reveal what was to come? Would the mystery of God remain hidden forever?

Then another voice spoke, rich with triumph. "Behold, the Lion of the tribe of Judah has prevailed!"

And John saw—

The Lamb, slain yet standing, bearing the wounds of sacrifice. And as He reached forth, the heavens thundered. The first seal was broken, and from the depths of eternity, the Horsemen rode forth—

White, red, black, pale—each one a herald of judgment, of conquest, of war, of famine, of death.

John trembled, his hands covering his face. The world reeled beneath the weight of their coming, and yet it was only the beginning.

The Throne and the Multitude

John was lifted once more, and before him stretched a sea of glass, clear as crystal, reflecting the emerald radiance of the great throne of God. Around it, the elders fell in worship, the fiery seraphim crying out, "Holy, holy, holy, Lord God Almighty, who was and is and is to come!"

And then a great multitude, beyond number, clothed in white robes, stood before the throne.

"Who are these?" a voice asked him.

And it was answered: "These are they who have come out of the great tribulation, who have washed their robes and made them white in the blood of the Lamb."

The vision blurred. The heavens quaked. John saw the dragon, the great deceiver, rise to make war against the saints. He saw the beast emerge from the depths, the false prophet speaking blasphemies, deceiving the nations. The world was given into their hands, and darkness spread across the earth.

But then—

The Second Coming of Christ

The sky split open.

From the heavens rode forth a Rider on a white horse, His robe dipped in blood, His name Faithful and True. His eyes burned with holy fire, and upon His head were many crowns. A sharp sword went forth from His mouth, and behind Him followed the armies of heaven, clothed in pure white.

The earth trembled as He came.

The beast and his armies gathered against Him, their banners raised in defiance. The kings of the earth stood ready for war. But John saw—there was no battle. There was no struggle.

The Word was spoken.

"Babylon the great is fallen, is fallen." And it was finished.

The beast was seized, the deceiver cast into the abyss. The kingdoms of the world fell before the King of kings and Lord of lords. The heavens thundered with a single cry: "Hallelujah! The Lord God Omnipotent reigns!"

John's Return and the Writing of the Revelation

The vision faded.

John found himself collapsed upon the floor of the cave, his body weak, his breath coming in gasps. His hands trembled as he pushed himself up, his mind still reeling from what he had seen.

A hand steadied him.

"Master?"

John turned, his vision still blurred. Prochoros, his disciple, knelt beside him, concern etched into his face.

John tried to speak, but the words caught in his throat. How could he describe what he had seen? How could human language contain the weight of eternity, the fury of judgment, the brilliance of glory?

Prochoros placed a scroll before him, dipping the quill into ink. "Tell me what you saw," he said softly. "I will write it down."

John exhaled shakily. He closed his eyes, allowing the remnants of the vision to settle.

Then, his voice barely above a whisper, he spoke.

"In the beginning . . . I heard a voice behind me, like a trumpet . . ."

And so the Revelation was written, the final words of the last apostle, the testimony of the one who had leaned upon Christ's chest, who had stood at the foot of the Cross, who had seen the risen Lord. The words that would echo through time, declaring not only what was and what is, but what is yet to come.

"Even so, come, Lord Jesus."

CHAPTER 18

Return to Ephesus & the Gospel of Love

The journey back to Ephesus was long, yet John felt no weariness. After his years of exile on Patmos, the familiar sight of the great city rising on the horizon did not stir his heart the way it once had. The grandeur of men had faded in his eyes. Only one thing mattered now—the love of Christ.

The church in Ephesus had changed since he had last seen it. Many of the first believers had passed on, and new faces now filled the assembly. Some came with burning faith. Others wavered, struggling against the pull of the world. Heresies had begun to spread, twisting the truth he had fought to preserve. But John was not troubled.

He had seen the Lord transfigured in glory. He had leaned upon His chest at the Last Supper. He had stood at the foot of the Cross when the earth trembled and the heavens wept. And now, in his final years, his only desire was to remind the church of the one truth that endured beyond all knowledge, beyond all prophecy, beyond all miracles: *Love one another.*

The Gospel of Love

When John spoke, his voice was soft but filled with an authority that did not fade with age. The believers gathered in the dim candlelight, hanging onto his every word. He no longer preached long sermons. His message was distilled into its purest form, the essence of everything Christ had revealed.

"Little children," he said, his eyes sweeping over them, "love one another."

A silence settled over the room. The words were simple, yet they carried a weight that could not be ignored.

One of the younger men hesitated before speaking. "Master, why do you always say this?"

John smiled, the lines on his face deepening. "Because it is the Lord's command," he said. "And if this alone is kept, it is enough."

He had seen all else pass away—kingdoms rise and fall, men strive for knowledge and power. But in the end, love remained. It was love that had held Christ to the Cross. It was love that had led Him to lay down His life for the world. And it was only love that would sustain them in the days to come.

The Lost Youth

One day, word reached John of a young man who had once been among the faithful but had now turned away. He had fallen in with a band of thieves who roamed the hills outside the city, and under the influence of their ruthless leader, he had become as hardened and violent as they were.

The news grieved John deeply. He had baptized this youth himself, had seen the light of faith in his eyes. How had he strayed so far?

Without hesitation, the aged apostle took up his staff and set out for the wilderness. His disciples pleaded with him not to go—he was too old, the journey too dangerous. But John would not be swayed.

The path was treacherous, winding through jagged hills where few dared to tread. The sun beat down upon the dry earth, and the weight of years pressed upon his shoulders. But he did not slow his pace.

At last, he reached the hideout. The thieves saw him first, emerging from the shadows with hands on their weapons, their faces hardened by a life of violence.

John did not flinch. "I seek one among you," he said.

The leader of the band stepped forward, his lips curling into a sneer. "Old man, you seek nothing here but death."

John held his gaze. "Then take my life," he said. "But first, bring me the one I seek."

The leader hesitated, then motioned toward a figure at the edge of the camp.

The youth stood there, half-hidden in the shadows. His face was no longer the one John remembered. The softness of youth had been replaced with something harder, something colder. His hands were stained with deeds that could not be undone.

And yet, the moment he saw John—his aged form, his eyes filled not with condemnation but with sorrow—something inside him broke.

He turned and fled.

John, despite his years, ran after him. The loose stones of the hillside shifted beneath his feet, but he did not stop. His breath came in short, painful gasps, but still, he did not stop.

"Why do you run from me, my son?" he called. "I am an old man, unarmed, weak. Do you flee from one who loves you?"

The youth stumbled to a stop, his back still turned. His shoulders shook, but he said nothing.

John stepped forward, reaching out with trembling hands. "Do not fear," he said. "I will take your sins upon myself. Only come back. Do not bring ruin upon your soul."

At those words, the young man fell to his knees. A great sob tore from his throat, and he clutched at the earth beneath him as if the weight of his sins could no longer be borne.

John knelt beside him, placing his hands upon the young man's head as he had done on the day of his baptism. "The Lord has not abandoned you," he whispered. "Neither will I."

The youth wept, his tears mixing with the dust. And in that moment, the darkness within him shattered.

He did not return to the city that day, nor the next. But when he did, he walked with John at his side—not as a thief, but as a child returning home.

The Enduring Word

Years passed, and John continued to teach, to guide, to remind. His body grew weaker, but his voice never faltered. The Gospel of Love was written, and through it, his words would echo beyond the years of his earthly life.

He had seen the empty tomb.

He had seen the risen Christ.

He had stood upon the shores of Patmos and received visions of the glory to come.

But now, as the days waned and the hour of his departure neared, he no longer spoke of great revelations. He no longer recounted the miracles. He simply said:

"Love one another."

And when his time came, he did not fear the grave.

For he knew it was not the end.

CHAPTER 19

The Vanishing Saint

The time had come.

John had outlived all the other apostles. One by one, they met their end—some crucified, others beheaded, stoned, or cast into the depths of the sea. He alone remained, the last living witness of the Lord's earthly ministry. But he was not immortal. The weight of years had settled upon him, and though his mind remained sharp, his body had grown frail.

He knew his time was near.

One morning, as the sun cast golden light over Ephesus, John called together his closest disciples—Prochoros among them. Their faces were filled with reverence, yet behind their eyes was the unspoken fear of farewell. John had prepared them as best he could, but how could anyone prepare for the loss of their beloved teacher?

He placed his hand upon Prochoros's shoulder. "You

must go to Jerusalem," he said. "Your journey does not end here."

Prochoros hesitated. "But Master..."

John smiled. "This is the will of God."

The disciples watched as John took up his staff, motioning for them to follow. He led them out of the city, away from the streets and the noise, into the hills beyond Ephesus. The road was familiar, worn beneath his aged feet, yet today it felt different. Today, it was leading him home.

At last, they arrived at a quiet place where the land was soft, untouched by the footsteps of men. John turned to them. "Here," he said, "you must dig."

The disciples looked at one another in confusion, but they obeyed. Taking up their shovels, they worked the earth, shaping the grave as he had instructed—in the form of a cross, as long as he was tall. The wind whispered through the trees, the air heavy with something they could not name.

John knelt at the edge of the open grave and closed his eyes in prayer. The sun bathed his face in golden light, and for a moment, he was no longer an old man but the youth who had once walked the shores of Galilee, hearing the words that had changed his life: *Follow Me.*

At last, he opened his eyes and turned to them. "It is time."

They stood frozen.

John reached for the earth beside him and let the soil fall

through his fingers. "Do not grieve," he said gently. "For though you will not see me, I am not truly leaving you."

One by one, the disciples embraced him, their tears falling onto his robe. Then, with slow, deliberate movements, John turned and stepped into the shallow grave that had been prepared. Lowering himself carefully, he sat, then lay back against the cool earth. With hands trembling, his disciples began to cover him with the soil. First to his knees. Then to his chest. John looked upon them one final time, his voice soft yet unwavering. "Love one another," he whispered.

They covered him up to his neck. He closed his eyes, and a thin veil was placed over his face.

And then, silence.

The disciples stood motionless, listening to the wind move through the trees. They had done as he had asked, yet something felt unfinished. They remained there for a long time, unsure if they should speak or leave. At last, with heavy hearts, they returned to the city, carrying the weight of their sorrow with them.

When they arrived, the other brethren gathered around them. "Where is the Master?" someone asked.

The disciples looked at one another. "We buried him," one of them answered. "As he wished."

A murmur rippled through the crowd. "Take us to his grave."

The disciples hesitated, but they led the brethren back

to the place where John had been buried. The earth had been left undisturbed, the grave still fresh. Yet as they stood before it, something compelled them to act.

With reverent hands, they removed the soil.

And then—they gasped.

John's body was gone.

Only his sandals remained, resting upon the earth where his feet had once been.

A stunned silence fell upon them. Some fell to their knees, weeping. Others stood trembling, unable to speak. Had he been taken, as Elijah had been? Had the Lord called him away in a way unseen by men?

None could say.

But from that day forward, on the eighth of May each year, a fine dust—fragrant and pure—rose from his empty tomb. The faithful gathered it, and it was said that those who touched it were healed.

His words had been true. He had not left them.

He had only gone where they could not yet follow.

CHAPTER 20

The Eagle's Flight

THE ETERNAL SAINT

The wind stirred over the hills of Ephesus, rustling the olive trees, whispering through the city where John had once walked. The last of the apostles had vanished from the earth, yet his words had not. They soared like the eagle that symbolized his Gospel, untethered by time, carried across generations, unyielding to the decay of the world.

His disciples, gathered in sorrow at his empty tomb, whispered among themselves. Some spoke of the vision of his body rising into heaven, while others, more cautious, simply marveled at the mystery of the missing saint. But one truth remained—John had not truly left them. His testimony endured, a living word etched not only in ink but in the hearts of those who believed.

The years passed, and his Gospel found its way into the hands of those who had never seen his face, never heard his voice, yet felt as if they had always known him.

The Words that Shaped the World

In the stillness of a monastic cell, an old scribe bent over a parchment, his quill moving with careful reverence. A single candle flickered beside him, casting long shadows upon the stone walls. He traced the sacred words with steady hands, whispering as he wrote:

"In the beginning was the Word, and the Word was with God, and the Word was God."

The scribe paused, his breath catching. He had copied many holy texts, but none moved him as these words did. They were not merely ink upon parchment; they were light breaking upon a darkened world. He closed his eyes for a moment, and in the silence, he could almost hear the voice of the apostle himself.

Somewhere in the distant deserts of Egypt, monks gathered in candlelit chapels, their voices rising in hymns inspired by the words of the Theologian. Beneath the high domes of Byzantium, bishops stood at the altar, proclaiming his Gospel to the faithful. In the vast catacombs of Rome, persecuted Christians clutched scraps of papyrus with John's words inscribed upon them, drawing courage from the love he had declared so boldly.

"God is love, and he that dwelleth in love dwelleth in God, and God in him."

Even centuries later, his words breathed life into weary souls, calling them to the truth, lifting their gaze toward eternity.

The Flight of the Eagle

The vision of the eagle soared beyond lands and ages, sweeping over the ruins of empires, the rise of new kingdoms, the prayers of saints who called upon his name. From the mountaintops of Athos to the gilded icons of Russia, from the illuminated manuscripts of Ireland to the fiery sermons of preachers who stood upon wooden pulpits in distant lands, the voice of John was never silenced.

It reached a lonely seeker centuries later—a man standing in a modern city, his soul weighed down by the burdens of the world. He picked up a worn Bible, opened to a page marked by countless hands before him. His eyes fell upon the words:

"I am the Light of the world. He that followeth Me shall not walk in darkness, but shall have the light of life."

And in that moment, he knew.

The eagle did not rest. It carried the Gospel forward, its wings stretched wide over the earth, its flight unbroken.

John had not died.

He had only begun to speak.

Epilogue

The voices of Saint John and the Holy Virgin have never been silenced. Though the years passed, though their earthly journeys ended, their witness remains, echoing through eternity, living in the hearts of all who follow Christ.

Saint John was entrusted with more than words. He was given the care of the Virgin Mary, the Church itself, and the temple of the Word made flesh. In that moment beneath the Cross, when Christ gave him His Mother, John received a charge that extended beyond himself, beyond time—a charge that would belong to all who believe.

He was the disciple who leaned upon the breast of Christ, who listened closest to His heartbeat, who drank deeply of the love that conquered death. And so, through his writings, his testimony, his Gospel, he made disciples of all who would listen, leading them not to himself, but to the One he had followed to the end.

And the Holy Virgin Mary, the Theotokos, remains not only the Mother of Christ but the mother of all the living, the one who leads souls back to her Son. Just as Eve once stood at the dawn of the world, ushering in the Fall, so too does the Blessed Virgin stand at the dawn of the new creation, ushering in redemption.

She who stood at the Cross stands at the gates of eternity, ever interceding for those who bear the name of Christ. She is the mother of the beloved disciple and the mother of all who take refuge in the Gospel.

Saint John has long since ascended to where his eyes once beheld the heavens opened. Yet his words still burn with light. His Gospel is spoken in every corner of the world, his letters still guide the faithful, and his Revelation still proclaims the promise of what is to come.

The call he once heard—"Follow Me"—did not belong to him alone. It belongs to every heart that longs for the Light, to every soul entrusted with the care of Christ's Body, to every disciple who loves.

Even now, he whispers the words he wrote long ago:

"Little children, love one another."

And the heavens echo his prayer:

"Even so, come, Lord Jesus."

About the Author

Robert John Hammond is an award-winning author, screenwriter, and filmmaker whose works explore faith, history, and the transformative power of storytelling. He holds a Master of Fine Arts in Creative Writing and has taught screenwriting at the graduate level, mentoring emerging writers in the art of narrative craft.

Hammond is the author of numerous books and novels, including *The Light, Transformed by Writing,* and *CB DeMille: The Man Who Invented Hollywood.* His extensive body of work also includes *American Orthodox: Finding the Ancient Faith in the Modern World, Light Journey: Encountering Saints, Miracles, and Sacred Places,* and *Voice in the Wilderness: Reflections on the Life and Legacy of Father Seraphim Rose,* each exploring themes of Orthodoxy, pilgrimage, and the lives of saints and holy people.

As the producer and director of the *American Orthodox* documentary, Hammond brings the stories of faith and perseverance to the screen, preserving the rich spiritual heritage of Orthodox Christianity in America. He also served as editor and contributor to *Roads Less Traveled: Journeys to Orthodoxy,* a collection of powerful conversion narratives.

His work in both literature and film reflects a commitment to uncovering hidden truths, honoring sacred traditions, and inspiring readers and viewers alike to seek deeper meaning in their spiritual journeys.